Drawing with Shapes Is Fun!

DRAWING A BEAR WITH SQUARES

Jo Marie Anderson

PowerKiDS press.

New York

Published in 2019 by The Rosen Publishing Group, Inc.
29 East 21st Street, New York, NY 10010

Revised Edition, 2019

Editor: Greg Roza
Book Design: Reann Nye

Photo Credits: Cover, 1–22 (background) piotr_pabijan/Shutterstock.com; cover, 1–22 (markers) Photo Melon/Shutterstock.com; pp. 5, 24 Daria Rybakova/Shutterstock.com.

Cataloging-in-Publication Data

Names: Anderson, Jo Marie.
Title: Drawing a bear with squares / Jo Marie Anderson
Description: New York : PowerKids Press, 2019. | Series: Drawing with shapes is fun! | Includes index.
Identifiers: LCCN ISBN 9781538331040 (pbk.) | ISBN 9781538331033 (library bound) | ISBN 9781538331057 (6 pack)
Subjects: LCSH: Bears in art–Juvenile literature. | Drawing–Technique–Juvenile literature. | Square in art–Juvenile literature.
Classification: LCC NC655.A53 2019 | DDC 743.6'978–dc23

Manufactured in the United States of America

CPSIA Compliance Information: Batch #CS18PK: For Further Information contact Rosen Publishing, New York, New York at 1-800-237-9932

CONTENTS

Bears have **fur** to keep warm.
Let's draw a bear!

6

Draw a blue square to start your bear.

7

Draw a green square
for the head of your bear.

9

10

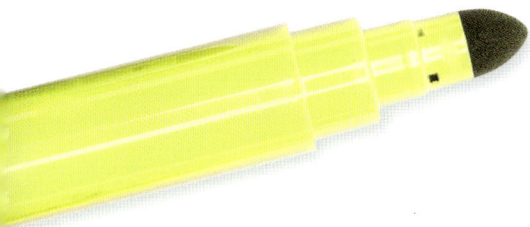

Draw a yellow square
for the tummy of your bear.

Draw two small purple squares for the **ears** of your bear.

13

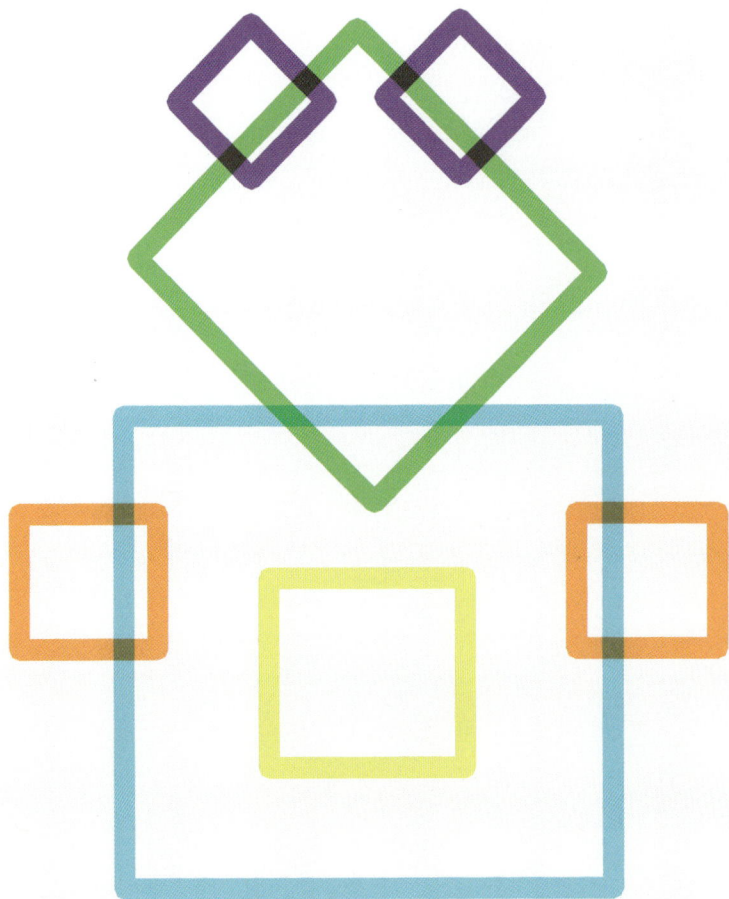

14

Draw orange squares
for two of your bear's **paws**.

Draw two pink squares
for two more paws.

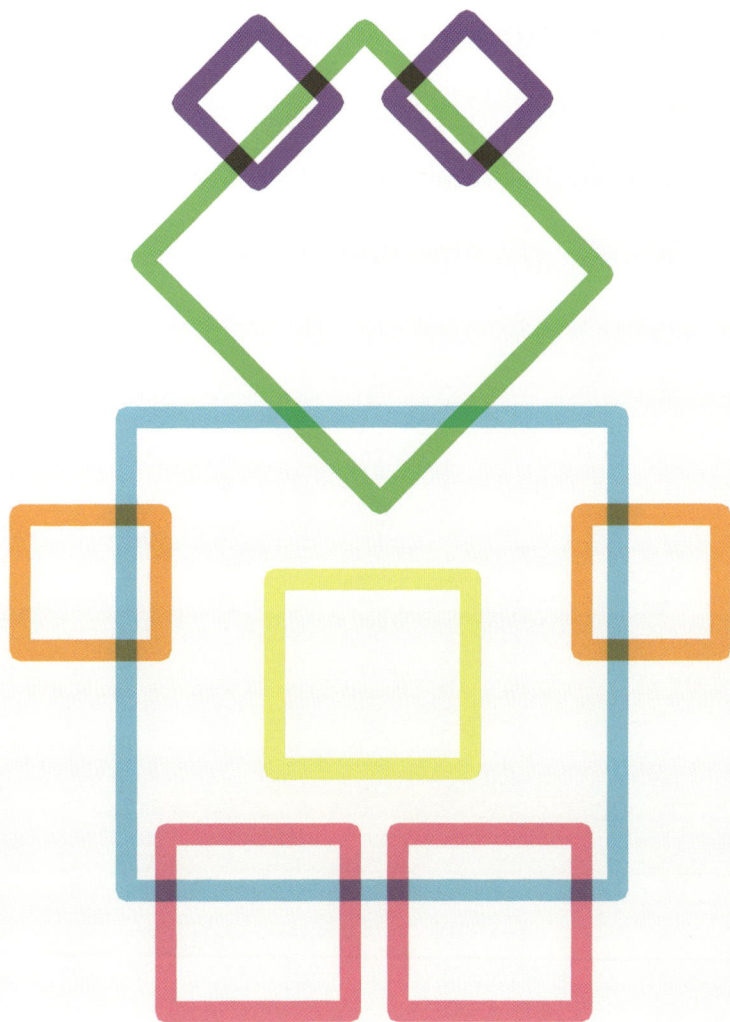

17

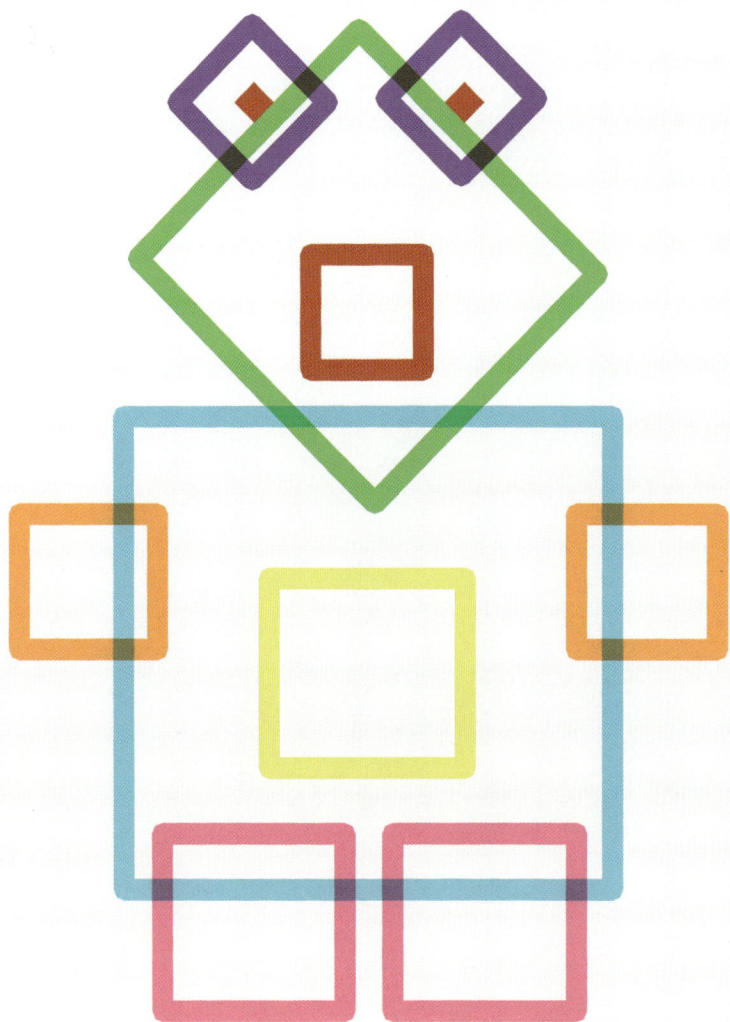

18

Add three red squares
to the head of your bear.

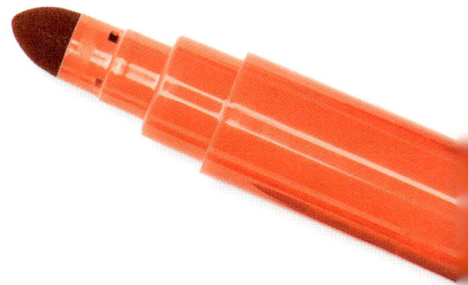

Add three small black squares
for the face of your bear.

21

22

Color in your bear.
Nice work!

WORDS TO KNOW

ear

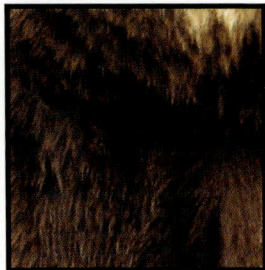

fur

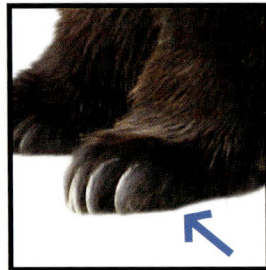

paw

INDEX

WEBSITES

Due to the changing nature of Internet links, PowerKids Press has developed an online list of websites related to the subject of this book. This site is updated regularly. Please use this link to access the list: www.powerkidslinks.com/dws/bear